# Where's the Poop?

by Julie Markes
illustrated by Susan Kathleen Hartung

HarperFestival®
A Division of HarperCollinsPublishers

Each little animal has made a poop.
But where's the poop? Can you lift the flaps and help the animal mommies and daddies find the poop?

"Little elephant calf,
do you need to make a poop?"

"No, Mommy, I already did."

"Fuzzy little cub,
don't forget to make a poop."

"Silly Mommy,
I already did!"

"My playful cub,
did you make a poop?"

"Yes, Daddy.
And now I feel
much better."